PETER PAN

the motion picture event

Adventures in Neverland

Also available from Pocket Books

Peter Pan: A Novelisation of the Hit Movie

Journey to Neverland

Welcome to Neverland

Peter Pan Movie storybook

PETER PAN

the motion picture event

Adventures in Neverland

By Scout Driggs

Based on the Motion Picture Screenplay
by P.J. Hogan and Michael Goldenberg
Based upon the Original Stageplay and Books
written by J.M. Barrie

POCKET
BOOKS

London • New York • Sydney

POCKET
BOOKS

Peter Pan: Adventures in Neverland
© Universal Studios Licensing LLLP, Columbia Pictures and Revolution Studios.
"Peter Pan" Live Action Motion Picture © 2003 Universal Studios, Columbia Pictures and Revolution Studios.
Licensed by Universal Studios Licensing LLLP.
All Rights Reserved

First published in Great Britain in 2003 by Pocket Books,
an imprint of Simon & Schuster UK Ltd,
Africa House, 64-78 Kingsway, London WC2B 6AH.

A CIP catalogue record for this book is available from the British Library upon request.

ISBN 07434 78037

Printed and bound in Great Britain

1 3 5 7 9 10 8 6 4 2

www.simonsays.co.uk
www.peterpanmovie.net

Contents

Prologue

Wendy Darling loved to tell stories, and she was very good at it indeed. Every night she would entertain her younger brothers, John and Michael, with exciting tales of great adventures. Nana, the large dog who was their nursemaid, listened too.

Sometimes, Wendy would tell of mermaids splashing in the deep blue sea. As it turns out, mermaids are not as friendly as one might think.

Other nights, Wendy and her brothers would pretend to be brave knights battling a dragon for its hidden treasure. Or maybe they would be called at the last minute to save the queen from a beastly creature with terrible manners and bad breath. It was hard to tell what the evening might bring.

But most of all, Wendy loved to tell stories about pirates. Wendy knew a thing or two about pirates.

She knew the names of all the most infamous scoundrels. She could talk at length about a certain battle that took place upon a particular ship. She knew many of the evil deeds for which pirates are famous. Most importantly, she knew all about Captain Hook.

Wendy often imagined herself aboard a pirate ship, sword to sword with the evil James Hook. She even imagined herself as the captain of her own pirate ship, battling Hook for a golden treasure.

On the night we begin our story, an even more extraordinary adventure awaited Wendy and her brothers. A magical boy was about to come into their lives.

The boy's name was Peter Pan and, with his help, Wendy, Michael and John were about to take the most thrilling journey of their lives.

1

Fly Away

On that special night, the stars were twinkling brightly in the sky, and soft moonlight was streaming into the nursery where the three Darling children were fast asleep in their beds.

Without a sound, the window slowly opened. Peter Pan and Tinker Bell quietly sailed into the room.

Tinker Bell, as you may know, is the loveliest of all fairies. To the untrained eye, she may look like a ball of light no bigger than your fist. But if you look more closely, you will see a magical creature with shimmering wings. And if you listen carefully, a soft tinkling sound can be heard whenever she is near. But who is Peter Pan? Why, he is a magical boy, and a bit of a rogue, too. He lives in a place called Neverland, where children never have to grow up.

Peter and Tinker Bell came into the nursery to get a closer look at Wendy. Peter thought she told the most exciting stories. In fact, he had been secretly listening to her stories for some time.

Perhaps it was Tinker Bell's tinkling sound that woke Wendy. She opened her eyes. To her surprise, Wendy saw a boy floating right above her head.

How grand, thought Wendy, *a flying boy*.

"What is your name?" Wendy asked him.

"Peter Pan," he replied.

"Where do you live?" she asked.

"Second to the right and then straight on till morning," he answered. The secret and magical island of Neverland can be hard to find.

"Come with me to Neverland," Peter said to

Wendy. He was quite sure that the Lost Boys would enjoy her stories very much too. The Lost Boys were Peter's friends. They also lived in Neverland.

"I . . . I cannot fly," replied Wendy, with nervous excitement.

"I'll teach you," Peter answered.

"Oh, how lovely to fly," said Wendy. She turned and looked at her brothers. "Could John and Michael come, too?"

Peter shrugged. It was fine if the boys came, but it was really the girl and her stories that Peter wanted to take back with him to Neverland.

Wendy rushed to her brothers. "John! Michael! There is a boy here who will teach us to fly!"

Michael rubbed his eyes sleepily, and John fumbled for his glasses. As the brothers awoke, they couldn't believe what they saw. There was a boy floating in the air.

"You just think happy thoughts, and they lift

you into the air," Peter explained as she showed them how to rise off the ground.

"Swords . . . daggers . . . Napoleon . . ." said John. He was trying to think his very happiest thoughts. But when he jumped off his bed, he tumbled to the floor.

Peter quickly went to Tinker Bell and shook a good amount of fairy dust over John. Fairy dust is a magical powder for flying.

Suddenly, John rose into the air. "I'm flying! I'm flying!" he cried happily.

Michael, following John's lead, climbed on his bed and revved up for takeoff. "Pudding . . . ice cream . . . mud pies," he chanted as he raced down the bed. Michael tumbled head first through the shower of fairy dust and magically rose into the air.

"I flewed! I flewed!" he exclaimed.

Then Peter blew more fairy dust from the palm of his hand. This time the dust covered Wendy, and she rose into the air, laughing with delight.

"Come away! Come away to Neverland!" urged Peter. "There are mermaids."

"Mermaids?" Wendy asked with astonishment.

"Indians, too," continued Peter.

"Indians!" gasped John and Michael.

"Pirates!" Peter said triumphantly. He knew that Wendy loved pirate adventures most of all.

"Who is their captain?" Wendy asked excitedly.

"The worst there ever was . . ." replied Peter. "Hook!"

The children couldn't believe it. Mermaids, Indians, and even Captain Hook! Their favourite stories were coming to life.

Stepping out of the nursery window, the children took off into the night sky. They flew high, skimming over rooftops and through the clouds. Higher and higher they soared, until all they could see were the tiny twinkling lights of the city far below. They followed Peter out over the ocean and towards the brightest star in the sky.

Suddenly, Peter threw his arms back and launched into top speed. The children held onto one another as they sped with him towards the bright light.

A boom could be heard as the children were swallowed up by the star. Then, after a short moment, they burst forth through a tunnel of light. In front of them was an endless calm sea. And rising from the horizon was the island of Neverland!

2

Meet Captain Hook

As you may have already guessed, Neverland is filled with many wonderful and magical creatures. It is also filled with scoundrels and brutes of the worst kind, pirates in particular.

As the children approached the island, they could see a pirate ship anchored offshore. But this wasn't just any pirate ship. This ship was captained by James Hook – the most wretched pirate of them all.

Peter, Wendy, Michael and John hid in a cloud high above the ship. Peter watched it through a spyglass. Just then, Hook stepped on deck.

"Hook!" John gasped as he took the spyglass from Peter. He couldn't believe he was seeing the legendary pirate in the flesh.

Captain Hook was quite a sight indeed. His hair fell to his shoulders in long black curls. His eyes were as blue as forget-me-nots, except when he was acting particularly evil – then they turned as red as blood. But the most frightening sight of all was the sharp metal hook attached to his arm where his right hand should have been.

"Let's take a closer look," said Peter, leaping onto a passing cloud.

At the same time, Hook tilted his own spyglass skyward. As he was scanning the sky, he noticed a strange-looking cloud – a cloud with the shadowy shapes of children inside. An evil grin curved across his face.

"Fetch Long Tom!" he commanded. Long Tom was a giant cannon. Hook was going to blow the children right out of their cloud! He rather enjoyed blowing young children to smithereens.

"There's some activity on deck," said Peter, trying to focus his spyglass. Before he could so do, a cannonball tore through the cloud, right next to him.

The huge explosion sent Wendy, John and Michael sailing through the other clouds.

Hook was disappointed. He didn't see the children falling from the sky. So he decided to take another shot.

Kaboom! Another cannonball tore through the sky. It punched right through the mainmast of the ship and missed the children in the clouds again.

"Blast!" screamed Hook. "Bring me those children!"

3

Shoot the Wendy Bird

Wendy was lost high in the clouds. She was beginning to wonder how she would ever find her way out. Then she saw a tiny, twinkling light. It was Tinker Bell.

Now, Tinker Bell was not *all* bad; in fact, sometimes she was all good. Fairies are so small, they have room for only one feeling at a time. Just then, Tinker Bell was feeling jealous of Wendy.

So when Tinker Bell saw Wendy lost in the clouds, she decided not to guide her to safety. Instead, she turned around and flew away!

"Tink . . .?" pleaded Wendy, flying after her. "I don't know where I'm going." But Tinker Bell just kept on flying.

Fortunately for Wendy, she was able to keep Tinker Bell in sight. Following closely behind Tinker Bell, Wendy finally emerged from the clouds. She looked down and noticed a lush jungle below.

On the ground, the Lost Boys spotted a strange figure sailing towards them.

"It's a large white bird," said Slightly. "Quite ugly, too." Slightly had never seen a real girl before.

Tinker Bell reached the Lost Boys first. "Hello, Tink!" said Tootles. "Where's Peter?" Tinker Bell flew close to Tootles's ear and whispered something not very nice.

"Tink says the bird is called a Wendy and Peter wants us to shoot it," Tootles explained to the others.

"We have our orders," said Slightly. "Shoot the Wendy bird!"

Tootles quickly sent an arrow whizzing through the sky.

From the air, Wendy noticed the arrow speeding towards her. Before she had a chance to escape, though, the arrow struck her right in the chest.

"I got it! I got it!" exclaimed Tootles.

The Lost Boys crashed through the forest to the small clearing where Wendy had fallen. She lay perfectly still.

"That's no bird," said Nibs.

"It's a lady," replied Curly.

As the Lost Boys discussed the strange creature that had fallen out of the sky, Peter dropped down behind them.

"Hello, boys! I'm back!" said Peter. Quickly, the boys bunched together to hide Wendy's body from Peter.

"Great news! I have brought you she that told of Cinderella!" Peter explained with excitement. "She is to tell us stories! She is . . ."

". . . dead," replied Slightly. The boys

parted to reveal Wendy's body.

Peter fell to his knees beside Wendy. He plucked the arrow from her chest and held it up in anger.

"Whose arrow?" Peter demanded sternly. Tootles was about to step forward when . . .

"Oooohhhh!" Wendy groaned. She was alive! The arrow had knocked her down, but it had hit the acorn she was wearing around her neck.

The boys were incredibly relieved. But now they realized they had no idea what to do with a Wendy.

"We cannot leave her out or she will spoil," said Nibs.

"Let us carry her down to the house," suggested Slightly.

"Wait! Is it sufficiently respectful for us to touch the Wendy?" wondered Curly.

"No. No, it isn't," replied Peter, noticing how dirty the boys' hands were. "We will build a house around her!"

The boys cheered at Peter's brilliant idea. They quickly set to work and built Wendy a lovely house with a door knocker and a chimney.

All seemed well – but where were John and Michael?

4

Ticktock, Ticktock, Ticktock

John and Michael were desperately lost. They trudged miserably through thick jungle until they found a dark cave.

When their eyes adjusted to the darkness inside, the brothers saw a ghastly sight – bones! The floor was littered with bones. Pirate skeletons were everywhere. Then, to make matters worse, they heard a sound . . .

Ticktock, ticktock, ticktock. The sound was getting closer.

Suddenly, a giant crocodile appeared! Its mouth was filled with razor-sharp teeth – the best kind for eating young boys.

John and Michael squeezed into a small opening in the wall and hid there as the massive creature slip by.

What the boys didn't know was that this crocodile was the most feared creature in Neverland. Even the pirates were afraid of it, especially Captain Hook.

You see, many years ago this same crocodile had eaten Captain Hook's right hand. Peter Pan had sliced it off in a sword fight and fed it to the hungry brute. Hook's hand was so delicious, the crocodile had been licking its lips for more every since!

Luckily for Hook, the crocodile had also swallowed a clock, which went *ticktock* inside it. Hook could always tell when the creature was near because of the sound. That ticking was the only thing that had saved Hook's life from his four-legged enemy so far.

Inside the cave, the crocodile became sleepy and decided to take a nap. It lumbered to a corner and curled up on the floor. The boys saw their chance for escape and quickly darted out of the cave.

The crocodile heard footsteps and immediately opened its eyes. With a mighty roar, the creature raced after the boys. John and Michael ran as fast as they could. They flapped their arms wildly, trying to fly.

They didn't get very far, because Hook and his men were waiting for them in the jungle. Watching from a nearby tree branch was the Indian princess, Tiger Lily, and soon the pirates had captured her, too.

5

The Mermaids

Wendy was becoming concerned about her brothers as it grew dark. *Where can they be*, she wondered.

Fortunately, Peter was very good at finding things that were lost. He knew the mermaids would have answers for them, so he took Wendy to the lagoon.

"How sweet!" Wendy exclaimed when she saw the mysterious creatures playing in the lagoon.

Wendy looked into the water and saw the glowing eyes of one mermaid looking back at her. Silently, a slender hand rose from the water and gently took hold of Wendy's wrist. The mermaid began to pull her slowly into the water.

"They will sweetly drown you if you get too close," warned Peter. He snarled at the mermaid, and she released Wendy. "But they do know about pirates."

Peter asked the mermaids if they had seen John and Michael. You can't speak to mermaids with regular words, though. You have to play a special set of pipes that only mermaids and Peter Pan understand. Peter began to play. Soon the mermaids told him all they knew.

"Hook has your brothers," said Peter, "at the Black Castle!"

*Wendy often imagined herself aboard a pirate ship,
sword to sword with the evil James Hook.*

*Without a sound, the window slowly opened.
Peter Pan and Tinker Bell quietly sailed into the room.*

Captain Hook was quite a sight indeed.

Hook was disappointed. He didn't see the children falling from the sky.
He decided to take another shot.

The boys parted to reveal Wendy's body.
Peter fell to his knees beside her.

Suddenly a giant crocodile appeared! Its mouth was filled with razor-sharp teeth - the best kind for eating young boys.

Silently, a slender hand rose from the water and gently took hold of Wendy's wrist. The mermaid began to pull her slowly into the water.

Wendy bravely rose to her feet and revealed her sword.

Inside a hollow tree were hundreds of glowing fairies,
dancing and spinning to a lively tune.

When Wendy awoke, she found herself on the pirate ship.

Hook raised his sword and looked directly into Peter's eyes.

For many years, Wendy would tell the story of her great adventure in Neverland... second to the right and straight on till morning.

6

Voices in the Dark

John, Michael and Princess Tiger Lily were being tied to a lone rock sticking out of the water that flowed beneath Black Castle. Hook had taken them as his prisoners to set a trap for Peter Pan.

The pirate captain was hiding high up in the castle walls, waiting for Peter to appear, but Peter and Wendy were already there. They had concealed themselves carefully.

Wendy could see Hook from where she stood. It was the first time she had actually laid eyes upon the dark figure who haunted her stories. He was every bit as rotten as she had imagined.

Meanwhile, Starkey and Smee, two of the most wretched pirates who worked for Hook, finished securing iron shackles on John, Michael and Princess Tiger Lily.

As the two crewmen began to row away in their boat, they heard a familiar voice.

"Mr Smee!" the voice called.

"Is that you, Cap'n?" replied Smee. He looked into the shadowy corners of the dark castle but could see nothing.

"Odds, bobs, hammer and tongs!" cried the voice of Captain Hook. "What have you done with those children?"

"We . . . we 'ave put the children on the rock, Cap'n," called Smee.

"Set them free!" screamed Hook's voice.

Smee was very confused. "Set 'em free? But what about yer trap, Cap'n?"

"Set them free or I'll plunge my hook in you!" threatened the voice.

What Starkey and Smee *didn't* know was that it wasn't Hook giving the orders, it was Peter Pan! Peter was hiding in the castle, throwing his voice in a perfect imitation of the pirate captain. Starkey and Smee were not very clever, as you can tell.

"You 'eard the man. Unlock them irons!" ordered Smee.

The pirates quickly undid the shackles, and John, Michael and Tiger Lily swam away.

Peter had made fools of Captain Hook and his crew.

Hook was furious when he learned that the children had been freed. He knew who was behind it, too – Peter Pan!

Silently Hook crept through the castle, musket in hand. Soon, he was only inches from Peter's hiding place behind a great stone dragon. He aimed his musket at Peter's back – finally, he would have his revenge!

"Peter, look out!"

Wendy's cry made Hook jump. He fired his musket but missed, and Peter Pan shot straight up into the air.

Hook unsheathed his sword. "We have him!" he called to his crew. A boat filled with pirates and a cannon emerged from the shadows. Then another boat with another cannon. And finally, the most fearsome cannon of all – Long Tom.

Peter swooped in on Hook, sword flashing. The pirate captain swiped back, first with his sword, then with his hook. His face aglow with an evil smile, Hook sneered. "The game is up, boy."

7

Wendy and the Pirate

"Yer gonna watch or fight, girlie?" snarled Cookson. He was quite an ugly brute, to be sure, but Wendy wasn't scared of him. After all, she knew a thing or two about pirates.

Wendy bravely rose to her feet and revealed her sword. "Who are you to call me 'girlie'?" she challenged. Finally, it was her chance to battle a real pirate!

Cookson charged at her. Their swords met with a loud clang. Wendy met each of his blows with one of her own. Then, with one precise swipe, Wendy slashed Cookson's cheek.

"I *am* sorry!" she apologised.

Cookson didn't accept her apology; he was a pirate, after all. Instead, he pulled out a pistol and shot the blade off Wendy's sword. Nothing was left in her hand but the handle.

Cookson began to close in on Wendy, but she was not about to be beaten by this boorish pirate.

Wendy took aim, threw the end of her sword, and hit him right on the forehead. Cookson went reeling backwards and fell off the high castle ledge into the water.

Wendy had defeated her very first pirate! Now she *really* had a story to tell.

Meanwhile, the pirates fired the two small cannons at Peter Pan. He flew out of reach, but there were no ordinary cannonballs. Attached to each was a rope net. Peter was caught! As he struggled to free himself, he reached for the dagger at his side. Peter sliced through the rope, only to find Hook standing over him.

"I have waited long for this moment," Hook

said with a satisfied smile. He signalled to his crew to fire Long Tom.

Wendy could not let anything happen to Peter. She grabbed a vine, swung through the air, and kicked the pirate controlling the cannon into the water. The cannon still fired, hitting the stone dragon. The dragon toppled into the water, taking Hook and Peter with it.

Hook pulled himself on to a rock. As Peter climbed up on the other side, hook grabbed Peter by the throat and raised his claw. "And now, Peter Pan, you shall die," Hook told him.

Peter merely smiled. He had seen something coming up behind Hook — something the pirate captain was deathly afraid of. Hook turned as white as one of his ship's sails when he heard the sound. *Ticktock, ticktock, ticktock* . . . the hungry crocodile was on another pirate hunt.

In his terror, Hook relaxed his grip on Peter, and Peter darted away. But Hook grabbed at Peter's ankle as he lifted into the air. Hook rose, too — he was clear of the crocodile!

But he wasn't safe yet. Peter flew low over the water, dragging Hook behind him. Smee rowed furiously after them in a small boat. The crocodile kept coming.

The pirate captain hooked his claw over Peter's knife belt for added protection. Peter unbuckled the belt, and Hook fell into Smee's boat.

Hook had escaped the giant jaws of the crocodile one more time but its hunger for Hook was growing ever stronger.

8

Fairy Dance

Peter and Wendy ran swiftly through the jungle and away from the Black Castle.

As they ran, Wendy noticed fairies darting through the trees. Then she heard music. Inside a hollow tree were hundreds of glowing fairies, dancing and spinning to a lively tune.

The music was light and sweet, and it carried all the way to the pirate ship. Hook heard it, too. He looked into the distance and saw the faint glow of fairies through the trees.

Captain Hook left his ship and followed the music. He made his way through the jungle by lantern light. As the music became louder, he parted the leaves to reveal . . .

"Pan! Dancing! With a . . . a . . ." exclaimed Hook. He couldn't believe it. It was his first look at Wendy. Who was this creature? There was no one like her in Neverland.

Tinker Bell was sitting on a nearby branch — more jealous of Wendy than ever. She tinkled something in Hook's ear.

"A Wendy? Oh, evil day! He has found himself a Wendy!" cried Captain Hook.

Hook wasn't entirely sure what a Wendy was, but if Peter Pan had one, he wanted one, too. Better yet, he would just take Pan's Wendy!

9

Red-handed Jill

Later that night, Wendy was sound asleep in her little wooden house. But she wasn't alone — the pirates surrounded her.

Following Hook's orders, the pirates lifted the small house and placed it on their shoulders. Then they carried it off through the jungle.

When Wendy awoke, she found herself on the pirate ship.

"Wendy, you are well, I trust?" asked Captain Hook.

"I feel rather frightened," Wendy admitted.

"Didst thou ever want to be a pirate, my hearty?" inquired Hook.

"Well . . . I once thought of calling myself Red-Handed Jill," she replied. After all, she *had* imagined herself as a pirate once or twice before.

"And a good name, too. We should call you that if you joined us," said the scheming pirate.

"What would my duties be?" asked Wendy.

"Do you tell stories?" Hook asked slyly.

"Stories? Actually . . . I have told stories about *you*," Wendy said, with a slight blush.

"If you were to join me, I should forget my vendetta against Pan," Hook lied.

"Why?" Wendy asked, surprised. She wasn't ready to trust this sneaky pirate just yet.

Hook replied rather cunningly. "No little children love me. I am told they all play at Peter Pan and that the strongest always chooses to be Peter. They force the dog to be Hook. The dog! I want to be remembered. I want someone to tell the *true* story of Hook."

Hook didn't really care if little children liked him or not. He was only interested in evening the score with Peter Pan. Hook knew that Wendy could lead him straight to Peter, but first she would have to trust him.

"Captain, might I have time to consider your generous offer?" Wendy asked. Of course, Wendy wasn't *really* considering becoming a pirate, but she didn't want Hook to know that.

Hook agreed, and Wendy was escorted back into the jungle. But she didn't remain alone.

Hook had the little house returned safely to the jungle as promised. He also sent something else to the jungle – a spy. The spy was meant to discover the secret hideout of Peter Pan.

As you can probably guess, it didn't take long for the spy to find the exact information he needed. Peter's underground lair was a very popular place, and so was Wendy's house. Someone was always coming or going.

With this new information, Hook sent a crafty lot of pirates to capture all the children and bring them back to the pirate ship. They were not to touch Peter Pan, however. He would take care of Peter himself.

One by one, the Lost Boys were snatched from their jungle home as they entered or exited a secret tree trunk that led to the underground hideout. John, Michael and Wendy were grabbed, too – everyone but Peter.

The children were all gagged and bound, and taken to Hook's ship, the *Jolly Roger*, to await their fate. This was a most unfortunate turn of events.

When all the children were captured, Hook squeezed himself through the child-sized opening in the tree trunk. Then he dragged himself through the narrow passageways that led to Peter's home.

He emerged from the darkness to see Peter Pan sound asleep on his bed. The unsuspecting boy had no idea of the rotten deeds at hand.

Hook stretched out his arm and slashed at Peter with his deadly claw, but he couldn't

reach him! Peter's bed was placed behind a wall
of tangled tree roots. There was only one small
opening through which to enter, and that opening was just wide enough for a child.

Hook tried desperately to reach through the
roots. He stretched his arm and slashed his claw,
but it was no use. He simply could not reach
Peter.

Then, Hook had an idea – a perfectly evil
idea. He noticed a small cup lying next to Peter's
bed. Hook reached into his coat and pulled out
a small glass vial. The vial was glowing with a
blood red poison. It was instantly fatal and
without antidote.

Hook was barely able to reach the little cup,
but he grabbed it and poured in three drops of
the poison. Then he disappeared into the dark.

10

Man Overboard

Satisfied that he had finally killed his enemy Peter Pan, Hook went back to his ship to finish off Peter's friends too. After all, this was the most enjoyable part of being a pirate.

Just as he was about to make the children walk the plank, there was a sound.

Ticktock, ticktock, ticktock – the crocodile again! The vile thing wouldn't leave Hook alone.

"Oh, the irony!" cried Hook. He was more than happy to feed all the children to the creature that hungered for him.

Hook shoved Wendy to the end of the plank, and she fell towards the water.

"The creature has swallowed her whole." Hook laughed. For a moment there was silence, and then the ticking sound began to move up the side of the ship.

"It looks for more, Cap'n!" cried Smee.

"Then give it more," said Hook, turning his gaze on the boys. "A banquet of children!" he cried.

Just then, the ticking sound rose into the air.

"Cap'n, it flies!" screamed Smee.

"All this time it was a dragon!" exclaimed Hook. "Hunt it down!"

While the pirates were busy trying to catch the flying dragon, something amazing happened.

Peter Pan secretly landed on the deck of the pirate ship with Wendy in his arms! He was alive. Peter hadn't drunk the poison Hook had left for him after all.

"Shhhh." Peter gestured, putting one finger to his mouth. He was warning the boys to remain quiet. He didn't want Hook to discover him – not yet.

Wendy cut the boys' bonds, and Peter slipped into the ship's armoury for weapons.

Meanwhile, the ticking shadow continued to cross the sails, and the pirates continued to chase after it. One brave pirate pulled back the sail just in time to see . . .

A ticking clock in the hands of Tinker Bell! She had been flying among the sails, casting a shadow that looked very much like a dragon. It was all a trick to distract Hook and his crew, so Peter and Wendy could free the boys.

Captain Hook couldn't believe his eyes – Peter Pan lived!

"So, Pan, this is all your doing!" screamed Hook.

"Aye, James Hook, it is all my doing," Peter said proudly.

Hook raised his sword and looked directly into Peter's eyes. "Proud and insolent youth, prepare to meet thy doom!"

11

The Final Battle

The great battle began. The pirates swarmed the deck ready to attack, but, to their surprise, they found all the children armed with swords!

Wendy and John were doing a great job fighting off a pair of pirates. Standing back to back, they each faced a foe. Then, with perfect timing, Wendy and John both ducked. The foolish pirates hit each other and fell to the ground.

Meanwhile, Michael had poor old Smee cornered. With the tip of Michael's sword touching his neck, Smee begged, "Please, lad, let me live." Michael agreed and let the cowardly pirate jump overboard to safety.

The Lost Boys were defeating the pirates one by one. Slightly counted each pirate as he fell, 'Six . . . seven . . ."

On the other side of the deck, Hook and Peter continued to battle. The captain was having a difficult time because Peter kept flying into the air, where Hook couldn't reach him.

Suddenly, Hook grabbed Tinker Bell, who was flying overhead. To his surprise, he began to float upwards as her fairy dust covered him.

With a shout of triumph, Hook rose higher and higher in the air after Peter. Their swords met with a clang. Peter angrily slashed, but Hook ducked. Peter furiously struck again, and their blades locked. Hook jabbed his claw in Peter's face, but Peter quickly swerved out of the way. Peter slashed at Hook with a lightning charge, but Hook blocked him again.

Hook lunged at Peter one last time before . . .

Ticktock, ticktock, ticktock. Hook looked down in horror. In the heat of the battle, he had floated away from the ship. Below him was only water – and the crocodile.

Hook began to panic, and since he wasn't thinking happy thoughts, he started sinking fast.

"Cannons . . . battle . . . looting . . . clashing . . ." chanted Hook as he tried to stay in the air, but to no avail. He continued to fall.

By now the crocodile was snapping at Hook's feet. Suddenly, the creature took a giant leap and swallowed him whole!

The children looked on in disbelief as the crocodile dropped back into the water and then spat out the metal hook onto the ship's deck. For a moment, there was hushed silence. Then . . . celebration!

The children all cheered wildly as Peter approached the wheel of the ship.

"Ready to cast off?" he asked.

"The ship is secure," answered John, with a salute.

"Then anchors away, lads! East by southeast!" commanded Peter.

A powerful wind filled the sails as a thousand fairies descended from the sky. The sails lit up as the ship lifted out of the water and into the air.

"Where are we bound, Captain?" asked Wendy. The ship was now sailing majestically through the clouds.

"For the mainland, Miss," replied Peter sadly. "For journey's end."

The clouds parted, and the glittering lights of London appeared below. Wendy and her brothers were home at last. Their parents and Nana were watching for them at the window.

For many years, Wendy would tell the story of her great adventure in Neverland. In fact, she told the story so many times she began to wonder if it really had happened. But then, out of the corner of her eye, she could see the shadow of a young boy or a twinkling ball of light, and know that there really was a magical place – following the stars – second to the right, and straight on till morning.

Peter Pan: Journey to Neverland

Discover how the Darling children prepare themselves
for their magical adventure with Peter Pan - practising
their sword-fighting skills and learning to fly!

ISBN: 0 743 49013 4

Peter Pan: Welcome to Neverland

Join the Darling children as the discover the Lost Boys'
underground hideout, meet Princess Tiger Lily, and sail
the high seas on the Jolly Roger!

ISBN: 0 743 49014 2

Peter Pan: A Storybook Based on the Hit Movie

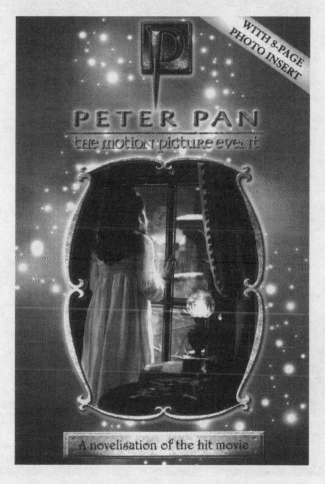

Live the adventure with this photo-packed storybook!

ISBN: 0 743 47804 5

Peter Pan: A Novelisation of the Hit Movie

Revisit enchanted Neverland in this novelisation of Peter
Pan - the film inspired by J.M. Barrie's timeless tale.

ISBN: 0 743 47802 9

All Pocket Books are available by post from:
Simon & Schuster Cash Sales. PO Box 29
Douglas, Isle of Man IM99 1BQ
Credit cards accepted.
Please telephone 01624 836000
fax 01624 670923, Internet
http://www.bookpost.co.uk or email:
bookshop@enterprise.net for details